PATHWAY TO POSITIVE LIVING

By Dr. Henry L. Causly

HENRY CAUSLY MINISTRIES, INC.
A NON DENOMINATIONAL CHRISTIAN MINISTRY

Order this book online at www.trafford.com
or email orders@trafford.com

Most Trafford titles are also available at major online book retailers.

Note for Librarians: A cataloguing record for this book is available from Library
and Archives Canada at www.collectionscanada.ca/amicus/index-e.html

Printed in Victoria, BC, Canada.

ISBN: 978-1-4269-1546-8 (sc)

*Our mission is to efficiently provide the world's finest, most
comprehensive book publishing service, enabling every author to
experience success. To find out how to publish your book, your way, and
have it available worldwide, visit us online at www.trafford.com*

Trafford rev. 09/02/2009

 www.trafford.com

North America & international
toll-free: 1 888 232 4444 (USA & Canada)
phone: 250 383 6864 ♦ fax: 812 355 4082

Contents

Life Is What You Make It 1
A Thankful Attitude 2
Change That Old Negative Thinking Habit............ 2
Sacrifice.. 3
Putting Your Best Foot Forward............................ 4
You're Special 5
Flexibility 6
Mental Pictures For Positive Growth..................... 7
We Have A Lot To Share 8
Thankful Affirmation... 9
Closeness To The Earth 9
Confidence 10
Relaxation 10
Putting Things Into Perspective 11
Positive Suggestions 12
Positive Attitude 13
Affirm Positively... 14
Affirmative Living.. 14
Awareness... 15
Perseverance... 16
Affirmation.. 16
Don't Be Afraid To Make Mistakes 17
Seeing Thought Patterns For What They Are 17
You have To Crawl Before You Walk 19
Enjoying Life Each Day 19
The Beauty Of Prayer 20

A Patient Attitude 20

Expect A Positive Change 23

Christ Sets Us Free 24

Your Labor Is Not In Vain 25

Why Your Labor Is Not In Vain In The Lord 26

God Is Love 31

Prayer 32

Optimism Thinking 33

Keeping Fit 37

Before You Start Any Exercise Program Consult
With Your Physicians First 37

Beginning Your Program 38

Body Stretch 39

Walking 40

Jumping Rope 40

Jogging 41

Push-Ups For Toning
And Strengthening The Body 42

How To Strengthen The Abdominal
And Lower Back 43

30 Positive Principles For Living 44

INTRODUCTION

There is a pathway to living a positive life. In this book we will explore spiritual, philosophical, and even physical principles that will guide you on your journey to a more enhanced and optimistic life. What are your thoughts about who you are? How do you feel about yourself? It all begins with you. "For as he thinketh in his heart, so is he." Proverbs 23 Verse 7. So, what you think about yourself is very important to who you are. In other words, if you spend the majority of your daily living thinking negative thoughts, your life will become a mirror of what's in your mind. Negative thinking will become habit-forming for you, like an addiction, and you will consistently find reasons to justify thinking and living in the negative. Have you ever met people who seem to never have anything positive to say about themselves, about life, or others. People who just seem to constantly dwell on the negative. I have come across many people like that in my lifetime. Many of us have family members and close associates who are always negative, and their negative thinking can affect us, if we hang around them long enough. You may wonder, how can a person think positive in an often negative world? You can think positive, because you do have a choice in the way you choose to think. "Be ye transformed by the renewing of your mind." Roman Chapter 12 Verse 2. So, how do we think positive in an often negative world? We must begin by transforming our old negative way of thinking to a new positive way of thinking. Old habits are hard to break. If you have been a negative thinker all of your life, allowing situations and circumstances to cause you to think negative, you must now re-program your mind to think in a new way. "Let this mind be in you, which was also in Christ Jesus." Philippians Chapter 2 Verse 5.

CHAPTER 1

Life Is What You Make It

Life will give back to us what we put into it. If we don't put anything into life, how can we expect to receive something out of it? While seeking better things for the future, be thankful to God everyday and fully utilize the strengths and blessings you presently have. Materially, and otherwise, you may not presently have what you desire. You may not have arrived at the destination that you desire in life. Despite your present circumstance, you must remember that life is a changing process. Nothing stays the same. Time brings about change. What do you have to lose by thinking positive through a negative situation? It is clear that thinking negative in a negative situation, is not going to help the situation, and certainly not going to make you feel better. Why not think positive? God is on your side. God's blessings has no boundaries, but we can limit ourselves and our blessings, by the way we think.

A Thankful Attitude

Do you have a thankful attitude, despite your present situation? Being thankful does not mean you are denying your present circumstance. You are thankful because you have faith that with God's help, you can rise above your present circumstance, and it all begins with your faith in God and how you feel about yourself. Just because you can't presently see the victory due to your current circumstance (whatever that may be) does not mean the victory doesn't exist for you. God foundation for operating in our lives, is through our faith in Him, through Jesus Christ. "But without faith it is impossible to please Him: for he that cometh to God must believe that He is, and that He is a rewarder of them that diligently seek Him." Hebrew Chapter 11 Verse 6. Faith is a positive word. Not a negative word.

Change That Old Negative Thinking Habit

God have given us a powerful mind. Our minds are so powerful in fact, that we can be in the midst of a negative situation, and through visualization, we can turn on the motion picture of our minds, and see ourselves relaxing on a peaceful island in the pacific. No other creature on earth is made in the image of God, except mankind. "And God said, let us make man in our image, after our likeness, and let them have dominion over the fish of the sea, and over the fowl of the air, and over the cattle, and over all the earth, and over every creeping thing that creepeth upon the earth." Genesis Chapter 1 Verse 26. So Surely, since God loved us enough to make us in his own image and likeness, we as human beings can change an old negative way of thinking, to a new positive prospective about life. We have the opportunity and power to not allow our present situation to dictate that we must (at all cost) think negative because we have developed a habit of doing so over the years. It's time to break the habit of negativity. It's time to unburden yourself with the load of negativity. You have the power and authority to do so. Give God your negativity, care, and worries. "Cast all your cares upon Him; for He careth for you." I Peter Chapter 5 Verse 7. Now, after you have turned all those burdens over to God, take a deep breath, a sigh of relief. Don't you feel better? Some of you may be so stubborn that you want to hold on to that old negative way of thinking. Let it go right now, turn it over to God. Release it right now, and be willing to say, "I can do all things through Christ who strengthens me." Philippians Chapter 4 Verse 13.

Sacrifice

To get something out of life there must be some sacrifices made. We must devote ourselves to reaching that goal. We must be willing to give up something to get something, both time and energy is invested when we make sacrifices and the amount of sacrifice depends on what we desire to achieve. For example, if you want to stay physical fit, you must exercise regularly. You may not be particularly fond of exercising, but in order to maintain a certain level of fitness, you must make the sacrifice to exercise regularly. If you are in school and want to do well on a quiz, you must sacrifice time to study. It works that way with anything in life. Sacrifice requires a devotion of time and energy to a particular objective. Each person has to determine the amount of sacrifice they want to put into something to accomplish a desired objective. If a person go into the military, they must complete Boot Camp. If a person wants to become a police officer, they must complete the police academy. These are part of the sacrifices, to become a member of these two professions. Each step we make toward achieving an objective in life involves sacrifice. Are you willing to make the sacrifice?

Putting Your Best Foot Forward

Each day presents new opportunities for all of us to grow in positive living. Positive living doesn't take a lot of complicated things, just a change of mind and habits from the old negative ways to a new positive ways, and since like attracts like, we will naturally draw into our experience the kind of thoughts and associations we are sending out. By putting our best foot forward, we make the best of every situation.

There are times in life when we experience negativity. No one is immune from such experiences. The way we handle the experience is what makes the difference. We can either handle the experience positively or negatively. We can either learn and grow from the negative experience and move forward or we can let the negative experience literally destroy us, which in the final analysis, benefits no one.

You're Special

It is important to feel good about yourself. Self-worth is a very important factor in positive thinking. You self-image personifies how others see you. How is your self-image? How is your confidence? Do you see yourself as being special? There's no one exactly like you on this earth. Isn't that something to feel good about? God made you so special, that you are uniquely made. You are not a duplicate. Your DNA, and handprints, are so unique that out of all the millions of people in the world, there's no one exactly like you. So learn to like your unique self. Take care of yourself. It's not selfish or arrogant. It's just common sense. If you don't like yourself, how do you expect other to like you. Live your life in a positive and purposeful way. Allow your light to shine, to allow others to see the good in you.

Flexibility

Being flexible in life is an asset that can help us move from one situation to another with relative ease. Flexibility gives us that necessary mental cushion that helps us bounce back when things don't go the way we want or expect. Flexibility helps us to understand that is up to each individual to accept the misfortunes life may present from time to time and learn and grow from them. Flexibility helps us to get along better with people by understanding that each person is an individual, and that we all have a right to our own opinions and ideas in this free society, as long we live our lives in such a manner to respect all human beings, regardless of race, religion, or national origin.

CHAPTER 2

Mental Pictures For Positive Growth

We can compare positive living to a person driving an automobile down the highway. In order for the automobile to travel in the desired direction, we must guide it by steering it properly. If we let go of the steering wheel, we will lose control of the vehicle, and not only do harm to ourselves, but other as well. When we have a negative thinking habit, we not only hurt ourselves, but we can often hurt others around us as well, and may not even realize the harm we are doing to family and associates. By steering the automobile properly we can guide the automobile where we want it to go and arrive at out destination safely. That is positive and is beneficial to ourselves and others around us.

Another mental picture for positive growth is the planting of a seed in the soil. The soil must be prepared for planting. Weather and soil condition must be right. The seed is then planted in the ground.

The seed doesn't grow and produce the next day. It takes time and care of the soil for the seed to grow and produce abundantly. In life we can remove old negative thinking habits from our minds and plant positive thoughts in our mind, and step-by-step we will grow in positive living. The more you do something the better you get at it. The more you think positive, the better you will get at it. Gradually changing the old negative way of thinking, to a new positive way of thinking.

We Have A Lot To Share

We have a lot to share with one another as human beings, and it all comes under one word Love. Love encompasses all the building blocks of positive living. "He that loveth not knoweth not God; for God is Love." I John Chapter 4 Verse 8. Whether it be peace, caring, trust, or understanding, love is the real foundation of life. What is God? God is Love. "For God so loved the world, that He gave His only begotten son, that whosoever believeth in Him should not perish, but have everlasting life." St. John Chapter 3 Verse 16. God the express image of Love, gave His only begotten Son Christ for our Sins.

Thankful Affirmation

Thank you Almighty God for my life on this earth;
Thank you for every breath of air I breathe;
Thanks you for the beautiful flowers and trees;
Thank you for the beautiful sky;
Thanks you for the birds that fly;
Thank you for the sun that shine;
Thank you for the rain that fall;
It's so good to experience it all;
Thank you for the love and friendship in my life;
Thank you for health, strength, and peace of mind;
To you almighty God, I give thanks for it all, whether it
be big or small.

Closeness To The Earth

Have you ever though about how important this
earth we live on is to our life? Every breath of air we
breathe, the food we eat, the clothes we wear, and
many other necessities come from the resources of
this great earth. All of the raw materials are found in
the earth and through man's knowledge of science,
he is able to produce products to enhance our
lives. Our very existence as human beings depends
on the resources of the earth. We are one with the
earth in both a physical and spiritual sense, because
the earth belongs to God. We are part of the earth,
and the earth is a part of us. The rain falls, the sun
shine, and nourish the soil with rich nutrients to feed

the animals and to grow fruits, nuts, and vegetables, we in turn consume meats, fruits, nuts, and vegetables, to maintain health and well-being. We are one with God's great universe. We have an obligation as human beings to take care of our planet. To enjoy the beauty of God's creation for our lives.

Confidence

Positive thoughts need to be practiced daily. When a person think positive. They reflect a sense of confidence that shows in their demeanor. People can sense the positive glow of a person who have confidence in themselves. A person with confidence is not afraid of life challenges. A person with confidence is not afraid to fail, because they use that failure as an opportunity, learn and grow. Everyone fails at one time or another in life. Our confidence in ourselves can sustain us through failure, to get up, dust ourselves off and try again.

Relaxation

In our frantic and busy world, it is important that we find time to relax ourselves. A visualization technique may help you to relax. First get comfortable in a sitting position. Close your eyes and relax your body from head to toe. Let go of all tension and worry. Take in a deep breath and exhale. Once you feel totally relaxed, allow your mind to become blank for a minute or two. Once your mind is blank and clear of all thoughts, turn on the motion picture of your mind and visualize yourself sitting under a shade tree in a beautiful park, with an array of beautiful flowers all around the park. You can feel a gentle cool breeze from the wind on your face. You visualize the beautiful blue sky, you can here the sound of birds in the trees. Your surroundings are peaceful. Just like the peace you feel inside. You are relaxed, so relaxed. You can also visualize yourself setting on a beach all alone listening to the waves from the ocean come ashore. Get comfortable in a sitting position. Close your eyes and relax your body from head to toe. Let go of all tension and worry. Follow the same techniques I describe for relaxing at the park.

Note: In order to complete the entire technique, read directions as necessary until you become familiar with the exercise. Visualize and relax for at least 10 minutes.

Putting Things Into Perspective

It is important to keep a sense of perspective about life, focusing on the positive attributes of living and not inundating your mind with negative thoughts. I remember being hospitalized for several days. I had never been hospitalized before in my life. It was hard for me to accept because I felt that that I had always taken good care of myself, but apparently not good enough care. I was lying on the flat of my back in the hospital, looking up at the ceiling wondering why me? I began to feel self-pity. Then after some thought, the realization came to me that self-pity was not going to help the situation. It certainly wasn't going to make it any better. No one is immune to sickness. Anyone can get sick. My change of attitude gave me comfort and peace of mind. I did not allow negative thinking (self-pity) to saturate my mind. I was determine to help myself as much as possible. What we think and how we think is a key element I believe in our healing process. Had I continued to pity myself, I would have been a miserable patient to be around, and this not only affect your nursing care but those who visit you as well.

Positive Suggestions

Look for the good in life situations

Learn to appreciate yourself.

Realize your self-worth and what you have to offer in life.

Be in your own corner.

Utilize your gifts and abilities.

Don't inundate your mind with negative thinking.

Use the tools of patience and persistence in your daily living.

Don't' allow anger to control you life.

Learn from your mistakes.

CHAPTER 3

Positive Attitude

The attitude we project each day determines how people will relate to us. If we have a negative attitude each day, people will probably try to avoid us. Could you not blame them? Who wants to be around someone that is negative everyday? If that negative attitude is hindering your relationships, where people literally try to avoid being around you, that is a clear indication that you need to change your attitude. Decide today that you are going to look at life in a more optimistic manner. You can change that negative attitude to a positive attitude, by making a commitment today to benefit yourself and others around you.

Affirm Positively

I feel good about myself. I am proud to live on this great earth, to share my life with others, no matter what race, creed or color.

I believe in myself, and in the things I want to do, because the Christ Spirit in me, will help me see it through.

I pray for a forgiving heart toward those who have done me wrong.

I know that I am going to make it in life, because I have faith in God and myself. Because where there's faith, there's always hope.

Affirmative Living

Each day we learn something new about life because the circumstance around us are constantly changing. Nothing stays the same. No matter how small the change, there is change. Just like the day changes to night and the summer changes to fall, we also must change. We get a little older and hopefully a little wiser each day we live. Living give us experience and awareness to aid us on life's journey. There are key elements in living affirmatively. The key elements are Time, Patience, and Persistence. It takes Time to accomplish any goal in life. No matter how small the goal, there is some time involved in accomplishing it. Patience is the relative of Time. They are closely related. Patience comes from within, whereas Time is a natural process that we cannot stop. Because Time truly waits for no one. We must use our Time wisely. We are as human beings are only allowed so much Time on this earth. The question is frequently asked, where does Time go? Time just seem to slip away so fast. The years go by so fast. The clock on the wall keeps on ticking away. The apostle James express it this way in the epistle of James in the New Testament of the Bible, "For what is your life? It is even a vapor that appeareth for a little time, and then vanisheth away." James Chapter 4 Verse 14. Treasure the Time that God have given you here on earth. Persistence the third element in Affirmative Living, means constantly working toward living a positive life. Set backs and challenges are all a part of life. When you face trials and difficulties in life, you must consistently re-commit yourself to live in the affirmative by saying, YES I CAN OVERCOME, WITH GOD ON MY SIDE.

Awareness

Try to become aware of how negative thinking can hinder your life and affect those around you. Make a sincere assessment of yourself, and make the positive changes in your daily living. Don't worry about past mistakes, because you can't change the past. Don't worry about being perfect, because none of us are perfect. You can start today on the road to a new and positive way of living. Just take it a day at a time.

Appreciate who you are. Don't compare yourself with anyone, because you are special in your own way. You have something to offer in life. Be aware and alert, because life is truly a learning process.

Perseverance

Perseverance is such a force of life that we cannot gain anything without it. Think about it. In everything you ever sought to achieve, there had to be a certain amount of perseverance on your part to make it come into fruition. Perseverance pays off. One must be committed to achieving one's goals. Although the odds may be against you. Times may be difficult. The road may be rough. Persevere and stay study on the case. Hang in there, and keep a positive frame of mind. Believe you can make it, and you will.

Affirmation

My mind is powerful, and I thank God for it. I can change a negative situation to a positive one by my thought and action. I am going to use this God-given tool to live a more positive life. No mater what situation I face, my only though will be that I will overcome it, with God's help. Realizing that all things take time, I will be patient while continually believing and working toward my true desires.

Thank you Master of the Universe for being the positive force in my life.

Don't Be Afraid To Make Mistakes

Life is a learning process and since life is a learning process, we all make mistakes. Life mistakes gives us experience which can be utilized should we face a similar situation again.   We should not lose confidence in ourselves because we make mistakes. We should try to learn from each experience.   Be it good or bad. Whenever a person seek new goals and ideas, they are going to make some mistakes, but that shouldn't discourage them from trying. You will never know what you are capable of doing until you try.

Seeing Thought Patterns
For What They Are

You are the master of your thoughts. Your thoughts can have no power, unless acted upon by you. There must be action on your part to make a thought tangible reality. So if you are thinking negative about something, you can see now that it is just a thought, a plain ordinary thought, one of many thoughts that travel in and out of your mind each day. A negative thought can have power over you if you dwell on it.   If you let it control you. Remember, you are the master of your thoughts. So, discard those negative thoughts that keep you depressed and worried most of the time. Don't give negative thinking power over you. Just treat it as another thought that's passing through your mind.

CHAPTER 4

You have To Crawl Before You Walk

For every accomplishment in life, there must be a starting point. We can begin living a positive life, by laying true foundation through our faith in Jesus Christ. We can start right where we are, and with what we presently have, moving forward at a comfortable but persistent pace. Everyone must begin somewhere. Start today. Don't put it off. Change that old negative habit to a positive one. You can do it.

Enjoying Life Each Day

You can enjoy life each day by looking for the best in each experience you encounter. When you achieve success, whether big or small, it is something to be proud of. Appreciate all of your accomplishments and thank God for giving you the inner guidance to achieve them. There are many things that can add pleasure to your life each day. Maybe you enjoy reading, sports, listening to music, hiking, camping or simply relaxing. Start today enjoying your life.

The Beauty Of Prayer

The beauty of prayer is that it is a spiritual gift that God has given us to contact Him. Take nothing for granted, pray daily. Here is what the apostle Paul said in his epistle to the Philippians in the New Testament of the Bible "Be care for nothing; but in every thing by prayer and supplication with thanksgiving let your requests be made known unto God, and the peace of God, which passeth all understanding, shall keep your hearts and minds through Christ Jesus." Philippians Chapter 4 Verses 6-7. When we pray, we may feel that we need an answer from God immediately because most people tend to be impatient. But God will answer in His own time. He already know our needs. He knows how to work out all things. That's why He is God. Omnipotent, infinite power. Omnipresent, universal presence. Omniscience, infinite knowledge.

A Patient Attitude

Do you have a patient attitude? We no doubt live in a frantic world. Most people are always in a rush.

There hardly seem to be enough time in a day to get all the things done that needs to be done. Despite the fact that we live in a fast paced society, we cannot change that, but we can change how we respond and react to these rapid changes. God have instilled in us a powerful positive tool and it's called patience. One Webster dictionary defines patience as "The capacity of calm endurance." I like the word "capacity" in that definition, it suggests that we are capable of this positive quality, that resides in us. But how many of us actually utilize this positive quality "Rest in the Lord, and wait patiently for Him." Psalm 37 Verse7. Here we are given essential instructions that after we have done all we can do in our humanness, then turn it over to God. Allow God to work it out. Are you willing to do that? God made a promise to Abraham saying "Surely blessing I will bless thee, and multiplying, I will multiply thee and after Abraham had patiently endured, he obtained the promise." Hebrews Chapter 6 Verses 7-8. As in the Webster dictionary definition earlier and in God's promise to Abraham, we get the sense that patience and endurance (two important positive qualities) compliments each other. "The Lord is not slack concerning His promise as some men count slackness." II Peter Chapter 3 Verse 9. What does this mean? It mean that when God make a promise, He will honor that promise. That's a positive quality that we can depend on, as we travel on this Christian journey. Dependability is very important in this uncertain world where some people may make you a

the Old Testament of the Bible, all the suffering Job endured, he still expected something good to happen in his life because of his faith in God. "All the days of my appointed time, I will wait till my change come." Job Chapter 14 verse 14.   in the midst of his trials, tribulations, and suffering, Job still had an expectation that a positive change would eventually come in his life because he trusted God. Job did not know when the positive change would happen, or how it would happen, but he had enough faith in God to believe that a change for the better would come. All Job had to do was hang in there.   "Weeping may endure for a night, but joy cometh in the morning." Psalm 30 Verse 5. Are you facing a job like situation in your life? Don't give up, and don't give in. Satan is a thief and a destroyer. "The thief cometh not but to steal, and to kill, and to destroy." St. John Chapter 10, Verse 10. Satan mission is to create havoc in your life. Christ mission is to give you a positive life. " I am come that they may have life, and that they may have it more abundantly." St. John Chapter 10 Verse 10.

CHAPTER 5

Christ Sets Us Free

In Christ, you are set free. Do you feel that you deserve the gift of freedom that Christ offer? If you have accepted Christ as your personal savior you are set free. "Stand fast therefore in the liberty wherewith Christ hath made us free, and be not entangled again with the yoke of bondage." Galatians Chapter 5 Verse 1. Christ took our sins and nailed them on the cross in His death, burial, and resurrection. Since Christ was willing to make the ultimate sacrifice for you and I, shouldn't you be willing to fully accept the freedom that Christ offers? By letting go of that old negative thinking habit because " If the Son therefore shall make you free, ye shall be free indeed." St. John Chapter 8 Verse 36. So, isn't it good to know that we can let go of past mistakes. We don't have to walk around day after day feeling guilty. "I, even I, am He that blotteth out thy transgressions for my own sake, and will not remember thy sins." Isaiah chapter 43 Verse 25. We may want to hold on to past mistakes, we may want to dwell in self-pity, but god lets us know that he have taken our sins away, and He have forgotten about them. Isn't that good news?

Your Labor Is Not In Vain

"Therefore my beloved brethren, be ye steadfast, unmovable, always abounding in the work of the Lord, forasmuch as ye know that your labor is not in vain in the Lord." 1 Corinthians Chapter 15 Verse 58. The Webster dictionary gives us some great definitions of labor i. e. physical or mental exertion, work, a specific task. So, we could say that labor requires action on our part be it mental or physical. Some labor may be in vain, but not our labor in the Lord. Like the Corinthians that the apostle Paul addressed in his epistle to the Corinthians, the work that we do in serving God is worthy labor indeed. As Christians we labor to build a spiritual building, a building not made by hands, but a building eternal in God. If you ever felt that as a Christian that your labor and efforts on this Christian journey is of no avail, I am here to tell you that is not true.

As Christians today, we can stand firm on the same admonishment that the apostle Paul wrote I in his epistle around A. D. 51 on his second missionary journey "Your labor is not in vain in the Lord." If you are a person who have not accepted Christ as your personal savior, here what you must do to be saved. " If thou confess with thy mouth the Lord Jesus, and shall believe in your heart that God has raised him from the dead, thou shall be saved." Romans Chapter 10 Verse 9. Read and affirm this phrase from you heart. "Jesus Christ, I now accept you in my life as My Personal Savior." Amen.

Why Your Labor Is Not In Vain In The Lord

Did you know that God does not change? "For I am the Lord, I change not." Malachi Chapter 3 Verse 6. Jesus Christ does not change. " Jesus Christ the same yesterday, and today, and forever." Hebrews Chapter 13 Verse 8. Friends will change, even some family members will change, but God does not change. "They shall not labor in vain, nor bring forth for trouble, for they are the seed of the blessed of the Lord, and their offspring with them." Isaiah Chapter 65 Verse 23. so when we labor in God, not only will we be blessed, but also our children.

When a carpenter labor to build a house, he needs the proper tools and material to get the job done. Wood, hammer, saw, nails, paint, and other materials. If that house is built properly and is built on a strong foundation, the carpenter labor is not in vain, and that house will last for many years to come. Jesus Christ is our strong foundation. " For other foundation can no man lay than that is laid, which is in Jesus Christ." I Corinthians Chapter 3 Verse 11. So our Christian labor is not in vain, because we have Christ as our solid foundation. Once you accept Christ as our personal savior, life does not all of a sudden become perfect, you will still face trials and tribulation in life. We live in an imperfect world. Christ said "In the world ye shall have tribulations, but be of good cheer, I have overcome the world." St John Chapter 16 Verse 33. Christ are telling us that even though the world is not perfect and even though our lives are not perfect, we can still be positive and cheerful in an imperfect world. We cannot fight this battle alone. We need Jesus Christ. Let's now deal with the seriousness of this spiritual battle. Satan is very busy in this earth realm. "And there was a war in heaven, Michael and his angels fought against the dragon, and the dragon fought and his angels, and prevailed not, neither were their place found any more in heaven. And the great dragon was cast out, that old serpent , called the Devil and Satan, which deceiveth the whole world, he was cast out into the earth, and his angels were cast out with him." Revelation Chapter 12 Verses -9. Jesus said "I beheld Satan as lightning fall from heaven." St. Luke Chapter 10 Verse 18. Satan and all of his followers was cast out of heaven into the earth realm. We cannot see them with the naked eye they are in the spirit realm. They are not flesh and blood. Since we cannot see Satan and his followers who was kicked out of heaven in the natural, we are at a big disadvantage in trying to fight these demons without God the

Father, Christ the Son, and the Holy Spirit, the Trinity. Here's what Christ said about Satan and his followers that are here in the earth realm, and what we should do as Christians, "Be sober, be vigilant, because your adversary the devil, as a roaring lion, walketh about, seeking whom he may devour." I Peter Chapter 5, Verse 8. Remember Satan main purpose is to "steal, kill, and destroy." But Christ came that "we may have life, and have it more abundantly." Satan is a taker. Christ is a giver, Satan is negative. Christ is positive. We are reluctant to turn to the local news these days for fear of hearing that someone has went berserk and shot and killed innocent people. We often hear of other weird and crazy things happening in our world. One thing we do know according to the bible, Satan and his followers was cast out of heaven into the earth realm, and they are here causing all sort of havoc. As we fight this daily spiritual warfare, we must prepare ourselves as Christian. None of us are immune. Here what the apostle Paul instructs us to do "Finally, my brethren, be strong in the Lord, and in the power of his might. Put on the whole armor of God, that ye may be able to stand against the wiles of the devil. For we wrestle not against flesh and blood, but against principalities, against powers, against the rulers of the darkness of this world, against spiritual wickedness in high places. Wherefore take unto you the whole armor of God, that ye may be able to withstand in the evil day, and having done all to stand. Stand therefore, having your loins girt about with truth, and having on the breastplate of righteousness, and your feet shod with the preparation of the gospel of peace. Above all, taking the shield of faith, wherewith ye shall be able to quench all the fiery darts of the wicked, and take the helmet of salvation, and the sword of the spirit, which is the word of God, praying always with all prayer and supplication in the Spirit, and watching thereunto with all perseverance and supplication for all saints." Ephesians Chapter 6 Verses 10-18. The apostle Paul admonish us that if we are going to prevail against the cunningness of Satan and his followers, we need to be prepared for a spiritual battle. We must be full armored. We must remember that we are not fighting against flesh and blood like our own physical bodies. We are fighting "principalities, powers, rulers, of the darkness of this world, and spiritual wickedness in high places. So our armor should consist of having truth in our hearts, the light of righteousness shining before us, and the Holy Bible as the gospel of peace.. our faith should be as Christians that whatever Satan and his followers send our way, we know that we will be able to deal with it because, Christ and his angels is on our side. When Christ was betrayed by Judas Iscariot (St. Matthew Chapter 26) and a great multitude of people from the chief priest and elders with swords and staves came to take him, Christ said "Thank now that I cannot pray to my Father and he shall (presently) give me more than twelve legions of angels." A legion is major unit ofthe Roman army which consisted of approximately 3000 to 6000 infantry troops. So, Christ could have summoned more than 72, 000 angels from heaven if he wanted to when Judas lead the multitude to take him. But He didn't, Christ gave His life on the cross for our sins. Angels are heavenly beings created by God. There are five division of angels: Seraphim, glory, burning ones. Archangel, warfare chief angel who contends against Satan. Cheribum, guards and protects God's throne. Living Creatures, worshiping and ministering angels, and Common Angels. God's angels is in the spiritual realm, and will contend on our behalf against Satan and his followers here on earth. Isn't it good to know that we are redeemed by the blood of Christ? " In whom we have redemption through his blood, even the forgiveness of sin, who is the image of the invisible God, the first born of every creature. For by him were all things created that are in heaven and that are in earth, visible and invisible, whether they be thrones dominions, or principalities, or powers. All things were created by Him and for him, and He is before all things, and by him all things consists." Colossians Chapter 1 Verses 14-17. God's word will strengthen and encourage you. So it's important you find time to study the Bible regularly. Get God's word in you. "Study to show thyself approved unto God, a workman that needeth not be ashamed, rightly dividing the word of truth." II Timothy Chapter 2 Verse 15. The more we study God's word, the more familiar we become with it. God's word will give you peace and comfort. We certainly need all the peace and comfort we can get in our frantic and busy world.

CHAPTER 6

God Is Love

What kind of God do we serve? We serve a loving God. A God who is the very essence of love. "For God is Love" I John Chapter 4 Verse 8. To show us just how much He love us, God gave his only son for the sins of the world. Would any of us been willing to sacrifice the life of their only child for the sins of others? That's pure love. "For god so love the world, that He gave His only begotten son , that whosoever believeth in Him should not perish, but have everlasting life." St. John Chapter 3 Verse 16. Since god love us so much, then we in return should love Him, and love one another. "Thou shall love the Lord thy God with all thy heart, and with all thy soul, and with all thy mind. This is the first and great commandment. The second is like unto it, Thou shall love thy neighbor as thyself." St. Matthew Chapter 22 Verses 37-39. We cannot limit God. We cannot put God into a box. God's ways are pass finding out

He is Infinite. We are finite. He is the "all wise invisible God the first-born of every creature." Colossians Chapter 1 Verse 15. God already know the experiences you will encounter in your lifetime. Since God is Infinite He knows the number of breath of air you will breathe in your lifetime. He knows the number of steps you will make in your lifetime. He knows all the associates you will encounter in your lifetime. What an awesome God we serve. How must we worship God? We must worship God in two ways, in Spirit and in Truth. "God is a Spirit, and they that worship Him must worship in Spirit and in Truth." St. John Chapter 4 Verse 24. How you live your life is a choice you must make. Will that be a positive choice or a negative choice? You must make that decision. It's left up to you. God have given you free will. Which pathway will you travel on this life journey? Will it be the pathway to negative living, or will it be the Pathway to Positive Living?

Prayer

Dear God, Master of the Universe that works through your Son Jesus Christ to bring about good in my life. I give thanks to you. I know that you are all powerful and understanding to your children, and that there's no problem you can't solve in my life. I know that I must want to help myself as much as possible. I am not perfect Heavenly Father, but find true comfort in knowing that you are, and that you are just a prayer away, when I need to call on you. Thank you for being a forgiving God. When I make mistakes you still love me. I am going to do my best to live a good life, to enjoy life and to make the best of each day. Amen. And So It Is.

Optimism Thinking

What is Optimism Thinker? An Optimism Thinker is a person who practice the habitual tendency or inclination to expect the best possible outcome or to emphasize the most positive aspect of a situation. This is a doctrine that Dr. Henry L. Causly and Henry Causly Ministries ascribe to. Are you an Optimism Thinker? Do you look for the good in life situations? Do you try to find some positive in the most negative situations? For example, there is a wise maxim, "I was complaining about having no shoes, then I saw a man who had no feet." Optimism thinking is an attitude of thankfulness. Here is a story about a man complaining about all of his troubles, having been laid off his job, and bills to pay. The man had a very negative attitude. The man went to the hospital to visit a friend who was dying of lung cancer. That hospital visit created a profound impression on that man causing him to become an Optimism Thinker through a defining moment of optimism.

That man began to count his blessings after visiting his friend in the hospital. The man made a decision to stop smoking. He had been a smoker for many years like his friend. He realized that it could have been him lying in that hospital bed instead of his friend. When the man left the hospital on his way driving home he saw, a homeless man, the man said that could be me, at least I am receiving my unemployment benefits, to keep a roof over my head and to pay most of my bill, and buy food, while I look for work. The man continue to drive toward home, then he passed a bus stop, where there were more than twenty people waiting to board the bus. The man said how thankful I am that I have an automobile. The man arrive home, and he looked at his children, and thought to himself, I am so thankful that my children have a roof over their head, a place to live and both parents are present in the home because the man thought to himself, there are many children from broken homes. It sometimes take one defining moment in a person life to turn them from a pessimism thinker to a Optimism Thinker. That defining moment for this man was visiting his friend in the hospital who was dying of cancer. The man come to realize that despite the trouble he had, he still had a lot to be thankful for, because he saw others who were much worse off than he was. Sometime in life we take things for granted. Many people allow themselves to get so caught up in negative thinking when they encounter problems that they have what I refer to as that " it's only happening to me" attitude. But a defining moment of optimism helps a person to see beyond their own problems, to a wider perspective of optimism thinking. Optimism thinking I believe is beneficial to a person's well being because it appear that people tend to handle stress better when they think from an optimistic point of view. Their attitude and demeanor is better. They have an expectation of hope. Pessimistic thinking I believe is not beneficial to a person's well-being, because it appear that such thinking tend to be dull and void of hope and expectation. Are you an optimism thinker? You can be. One sure way to be an optimism thinker is to count your blessing each day. God allowed you to wake up to see a brand new day. You should be grateful. Many did not live to see this day. Many are lying up in a hospital bed. When we take our minds off ourselves, and focus on God through prayer and thanksgiving for all of His blessing we are on the road to being optimism thinkers. When we are in an optimistic frame of mind, we are more loving, more giving, we smile more, and easier to be around. I was managing some employees at a large hospital in Los Angeles, California. One of the employees, would never smile. Some of the visitors and employees who entered the hospital started to complain, that the employee never greeted them with a smile when they entered the hospital. I called the employee into my office for counseling. I informed him that there were complaints from visitors and employees that he never smile and greet them when they entered the hospital. The employee told me that he never smile. I ask him why not? The employee excuse was that he has been that way since he was young. I told the employee that he is in customer service, and that a smile goes a long way in fostering good

CHAPTER 7

Keeping Fit

In the next few pages I want to address some simple and inexpensive ways to keep physically fit. Just as we think positive, we want to keep our bodies fit to enhance our overall well-being, and to help release some of the stresses of life. Because our mental, spiritual, and physical well-being are all connected and is a part of our total being. You don't need a lot of expensive exercise equipment to stay fit. What you need is the desire to be fit, and the motivation to take action to make it happen.

Before You Start Any Exercise Program Consult With Your Physicians First.

Keeping fit and feeling well is very important in our hectic society. We live in a stressed oriented society, and it is important that we find constructive, healthy, ways to let go of stress and tension. Exercise is a great stress and tension reliever. It helps to calm the mind, improve the cardiovascular system, helps tone the body, and enhances one overall well being, when done on a regular and consistent basis. Keeping Fit doesn't have to be costly. In fact, it can be quite economical. The most important thing when you start your fitness program is to be discipline about it. You must remember that the one person you can depend on is yourself. So when your exercise partner decide not to participate on a regular basis, by making all kind of excuses, you must have the discipline to stay regular with your exercise program. You will reap the benefits. If you are ill, is not to exercise until you are felling better. Never make your fitness program become a bore. Enjoy it. Have fun. Remember, you are doing something to benefit yourself. Keep a positive attitude. Now, lets get on the road to keeping fit.

Beginning Your Program

Your approach to staying fit is very important particularly if you have been an inactive person most of your life. You must approach a fitness program sensibly, and you should maintain a routine or plan and stay with it. No matter how busy you are, create some time in your busy schedule for self. If you only have time to exercise twenty minutes a day, that's better than not doing anything at all. So, find a time between the time you get out of bed in the mornings and before you go to bed at night to do something for self. Exercise is for your benefit.

Before you start any exercise program, warm-up first. Warm-up consist of stretching and moving the body in an even smooth motion to help reduce the chance of strain or pulling a muscle after you begin you exercise routine. Use common sense when warming up. Don't over do it . Use the same common sense while doing your exercise routine. Whether you are a business person on the go, a busy housewife, or a student, you owe it to yourself to keep fit. Don't put it off start

today.

Body Stretch

Spread your feet about shoulder width apart, reach both hands toward the ceiling, or if outside toward the sky, with fingers extended. Gently stretch for about 30 seconds. Repeat 10 times. Keeping your feet spread shoulder width apart, reach down in a gentle manner (slightly bend your knees if necessary) touching your toes. Repeat 10 times. Hold about 30 seconds. Repeat 10 times.

Lay on the floor or ground on your back. Extend both arms above your head. Extend your fingers. Gently stretch the entire body. Concentrate on feeling the stretch in your toes, calves, thighs, shoulders, arm and fingers. Hold stretch for about 30 seconds. Repeat 10 times. Now, sit up and gently touch your toes with both hands (bend your knees if necessary) feel the stretch in your waist, buttocks, hamstring, calves, shoulder, arms, and back. Repeat 10 times.

Walking

If you have been a sedentary person most of your life, and was never motivated to exercise on a regular basis, I suggest you start with a low impact exercise such as walking. Walking is natural, and does not create as much tension and stress muscles as more vigorous exercises such as jogging or tennis. Walking is economical. All you need is a comfortable pair of tennis shoes and clothing. You can begin your fitness program by walking around the block in your neighborhood, or walking at a local park or at the beach.. start your walking program at a slow pace for the several day then begin to increase your pace as you stamina increases. Walk 30 to 45 minutes at least three times a week.

Jumping Rope

Jumping rope is a very convenient and inexpensive way to keep fit. You can purchase a jump rope at your local sports store. If you have never jumped rope before, it may take a little time before you develop your coordination to maintain a steady rhythm. After a few practice sessions, you will get the knack of it. If your work schedule takes you from city to city, pack your jump rope in your luggage, then you can jump rope in your hotel room for five to ten minutes a day. Some other convenient and inexpensive aerobics you can do in your hotel room are walking in place, jogging in place, and jumping jacks. These exercises are particularly convenient during inclement weather, or when you are on the go and don't have time to visit a gym to keep fit.

Jogging

Jogging, like all of the exercises I have mentioned can be inexpensive and convenient. I stress again, you don't need expensive equipment to keep fit.

Whether you like exercising with someone, or exercising alone, these exercises offers a simple inexpensive approach to fitness. I enjoy the fact that I have the discipline to exercise on a regular basis. Regular to me is at least three times a week. . You must depend on yourself to keep fit. I enjoy walking or jogging at a park, beach, college of high school track field. You must choose the best location that suits you to do your jogging. Never jog in unsafe areas, or where there are crowded vehicle traffic conditions. Finally, have a common sense approach about your jogging program. Don't over do it. You are not trying to win a marathon. You are trying to stay fit, and have fun doing it. Start your jogging routine to what's comfortable for you, at about 15 minutes and work up as your stamina increases. Remember to consult with your physician before you begin any exercise program.

Push-Ups For Toning And Strengthening The Body

If you do not have the upper body strength to do full push-ups, begin with modified push-ups. Lay on the floor on your stomach. Place the palm of your hand flat on the floor near your shoulders, about shoulder width apart. In a smooth even motion, leaving your knees on the floor, push the upper body up until both arms are straight at the elbow. (Do not strain your lower back. Hold for one or two seconds and then back down. Do three sets of 10 each. Increase repetitions as your strength increase.

To do full push-ups, lay on the floor on your stomach. Place the palm of your hands flat on the floor, near your shoulders, about shoulder width apart. Put both feet together with toes against the floor. In a slow easy motion, keeping your body straight and stiff (do not strain lower back) push your entire body up from the floor until both arms are straight at the elbow. Hold for one or two seconds and then back down. Do three sets of ten. Increase repetitions as your strength increases.

How To Strengthen The Abdominal And Lower Back

Sit-ups and leg lifts are good exercises to strengthen the abdominal and lower back. If you don't have a back problem, you van begin by doing modified sit-ups and leg lifts.

For modified sit-ups lay on your back. Bend your knees. Place both hands behind your head with fingers clasped. In a smooth easy motion, lift your head about two inches from the floor or ground, and then back down. Bend your knees if necessary. Do two sets, 15 repetitions each. Follow the same steps in doing full sit-ups, except in a smooth easy motion lift your head up until you elbows touch both knees, and then back down. Bend you knees if necessary.

For modified leg lifts lay on your back. Bend your knees. Place both hands behind your head with fingers clasped. Ina smooth easy motion, lift your legs up about two inches from the floor or ground and then back down. Do two sets 15, repetitions each. Follow the same procedure for doing full leg lifts, except to keep both legs straight.

30 Positive Principles
For Living

1. I am somebody.

2. I am loved and love all mankind.

3. I love life.

4. I feel good about myself.

5. I respect others and myself.

6. I will not abuse or misuse my mind and body.

7. I have a good attitude about life.

8. I can overcome failures and obstacles.

9. I am a dependable person.

10. I have dedication.

11. I have determination.

12. I have confidence in myself.

13. I have courage.

14. I have patience.

15. I have endurance.

16. I realize that mistakes, setbacks, failures, and obstacles occasionally happens in life, but with an optimistic attitude and a desire to succeed, I will overcome them.

17. I am healthy.

18. I am becoming more successful and prosperous.

19. I have faith in myself.

20. I trust myself.

21. I have a good self-image.

22. I am becoming a more dynamic, asservative and articulate person.

23. I can feel a sense of calm and peace inside me , even though my surrounding may be turbulent.

24. I am not afraid of life.

25. I am unique and special, because there is no one in this world exactly like me.

26. I can change a negative situation into a positive one by changing my thoughts and actions.

27. Life is a growing and learning process, so therefore I will learn from my mistakes.

28. I am going to appreciate myself, accept myself, and be the best person i can be because I am my own best friend.

29. The world is beautiful and I thank God for giving me the gift of life to experience living.

30. So, I have a lot to be joyous and happy about each and every day I arise.